Mooseltoe

Margie Palatini

Illustrated by Henry Cole

SCHOLASTIC INC.
New York Toronto London Auckland Sydney
Mexico City New Delhi Hong Kong Buenos Aires

ISBN 0-439-33040-8

Published by Scholastic Inc., 555 Broadway, New York, NY 10012, by arrangement with Hyperion Books for Children, an imprint of Disney Children's Book Group, LLC.

29 28 27 26 9/0

Printed in the U.S.A. 40

First Scholastic printing, November 2001

This book is set in 16-pt. Meridian.

For Francine,
who is always "perfectly perfect"
—M.P.

To Katherine,
who makes every day feel like Christmas
With love,
Hen

WINTER
NDERLAN

'Twas the season,

and Moose was merry.

He joyfully tickled the ivories with a tuneful of tidings and a flurry of fa la la's. He was so full of ho ho ho's, even his moosetache had the holiday spirit!

But Moose was more than just a bit merry and bright.

He was busy, busy, busy. There was a lot to be done on his list of to-do's.

But—with orderly organization, a bit of regimentation, lots of imagination, and just plain old Moose know-how—getting ready for the big day should have been simple. Easy. Yes, in all probability, just . . .

perfectly perfect.

He wasted not one merry minute. Moose got movin' and put some hustle into the holiday bustle. He went to work.

He wrote cards and letters till his hooves hurt.

Check.

He shopped till he dropped.

Check.

He hauled home boxes and bags and presents galore. Moose had gifts for everyone stacked from ceiling to floor.

Check. Check. Check.

Then he wrapped. Yo. Yo. Yo.

And he ribboned. Ho. Ho. Ho.

And on each and every package he tied a big, beautiful bow.

Check and **double check.** So far . . . so simple. So easy. So . . .

perfectly perfect.

Another look at the list, and Moose headed for the kitchen. He pulled out the pots, pans, and bowls. Sifted through stacks and racks of cookbooks. He whisked with his left. Spooned with his right.

Moose baked tons of tins of cookies.

Check.

Dozens of cakes, breads, and sweets.

Check. Check. Check.

He made jellies. Sticky jams.

Moose roasted a goose and some chestnuts. He toasted marshmallows and yams.

Check. Check. Check.

Triple check.

Yes. Yes. So simple. So easy.

And, but of course, so

perfectly perfect.

Decorations were up next on his list of things to do and get done.

So Moose decked the halls.

Then spruced up the walls.

He beaded, bowed, and mooseltoed.

He gathered garlands. Roped wreaths and holly. Jingled bells. Sang Noels—oh, good golly, this moose was jolly.

Check. Check. Check. Check. Check. Check . . . Check.

Last, but not least, he hung all the stockings, each and every one, with special care. And just in time, too. Soon Santa would be there.

Check and **final check.**

Yessiree. Getting ready for Christmas was an absolute snap. And so simple. So easy. And if he did say so himself, Moose thought, totally, utterly, completely . . .

perfectly perfect.

On that night before Christmas, Mother, little Sissy, Bucky, and Junior looked all through the house. What a job Moose had done! Everything looked bountiful. Festive. Quite fine, indeed.

There was just one minor problem, if you will.

"Oh, dear," sighed the Mrs. as the five stared at one empty corner. "Oh, my. Oh, me. Oh, gee."

"Pop! What happened?" cried Junior. "You forgot the tree!"

Ooops! Where would they hang the tinsel? String the popcorn? Light the lights? Where would Santa leave his gifts for the kiddies on Christmas Eve night?

So Moose pulled on his galoshes and put on his hat. He would find a tree **somewhere**—somehow. And that's all there was to that.

So, out went the moose, braving blustery blowing winds and the cold. Trudging through snowdrifts, courageous and bold.

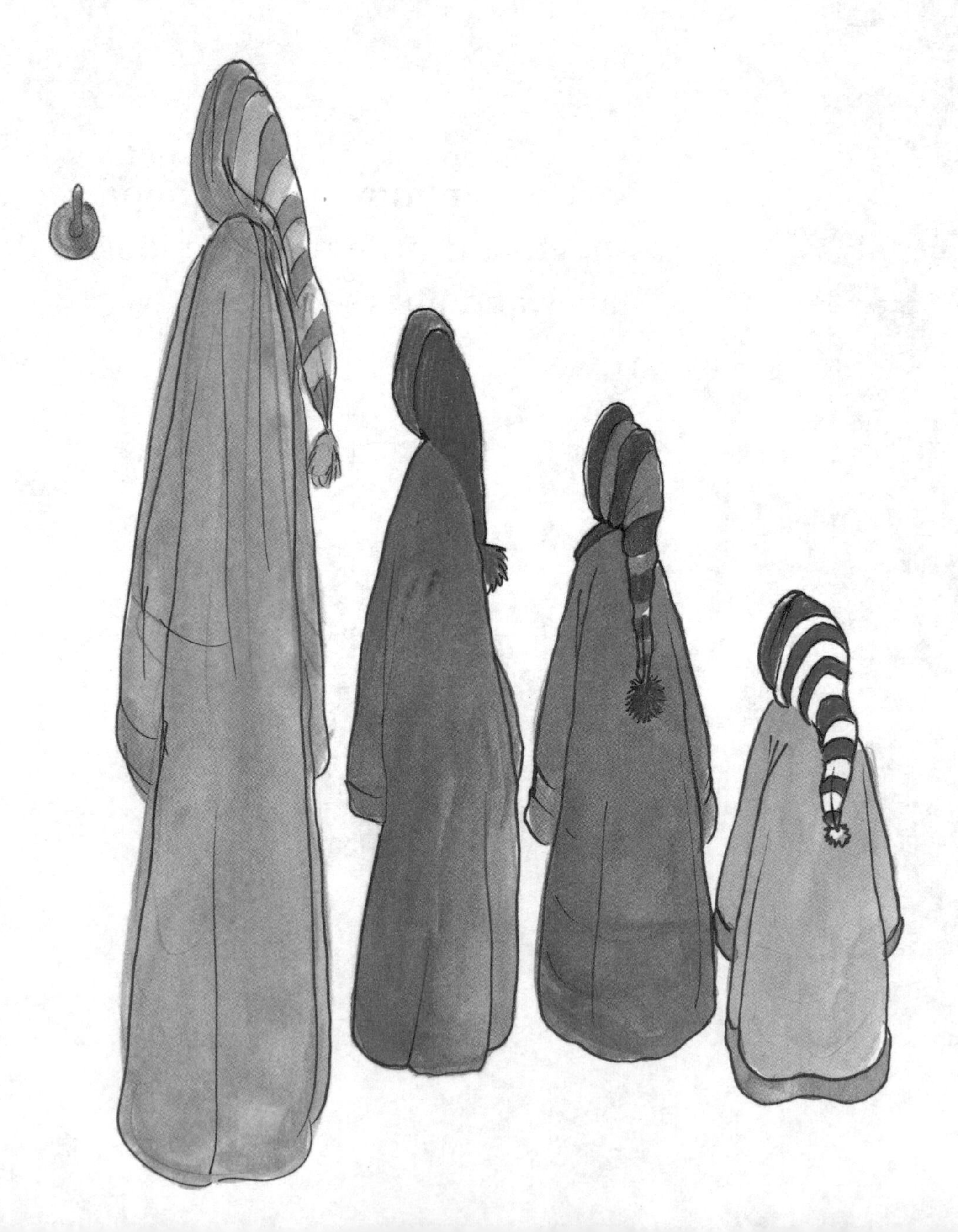

Moose first hoofed it down to the corner. Not a tree to be had.

Then he slid around the block.

Uh-oh.

Things were looking bad.

He went down every boulevard, street, and little road. He looked down lanes and alleys. . . .

Every tree had been sold.

There wasn't a branch, not a twig, not even one lousy bowless bough hanging around.

Nope. Nada. Nothing.

Not a tree to be found.

"No tree," sighed a sad Moose as he came home empty-handed that snowy eve.

The kids tried to make the best of it. They said, "Oh, so, who needs a tree?" But Moose could plainly see they were short on the glee.

He knew he had to do something. And that's just what he did.

In the empty corner he stood and spread his arms out very wide. Then he smiled at his children. And he winked at his bride.

"Kids," he declared. "Fetch your forgetful pop some of that tried-and-true family glop."

So back came
the kids carrying a
big pot of glue. And without a
word to one another, they
knew just what to do.

They
each took a part.
Grabbing strands. Taking hold. Then
carefully . . . oh, so carefully . . .
they glopped.
And they plopped.
They pasted.
And they pressed.

They curled and
twirled every which
way a follicle
could fathom,

until
Moose's magnificent
moosetache . . . was indeed even
more of a marvel to see.

Moose was just a few needles shy of being an evergreen tree! They strung Moose with lights from his head to his toes. And draped him with tinsel, beginning right with his nose.

They hung balls that were shiny. And bells that twinkled. Candy canes, berries, and plums sugar-sprinkled. Then—they all stood back—Junior plugged in his pop.

"Oooooooh. Aaaaaah."

Yes, Moose truly was one incredible sight. He was glorious and glowing. And boy, oh boy, was he ever bright!

Then Junior placed the star on top of Moose's head. He gave him a kiss. And a pat. And they all headed off to bed.

Except Moose, of course.

He stayed in the corner instead. Still twinkling. And blinking. And waiting for Santa.

Oh . . . so it wasn't so simple. And it wasn't so easy. And **okay, okay,** it wasn't so

But do you know what? . . .

It was pretty close.

Ho! Ho! Ho!